D1477971

Billy Bully Bug
(Learns a Lesson in Hawaii.

Sincere thanks from Mrs. B and Miss Jodi:

For Kerry Jackson, our musical director who came into this world a child prodigy. You are an extraordinary talent who has taken the voices, ideas, music and imagination of one woman and grown them into magically fun and amazingly entertaining pieces of work. You are overworked and underpaid, admired and beloved. You have loaned your remarkable gifts to this project selflessly and without thought to gain. Because of you, we are bringing stories, lessons and laughter to children right where they are. And, we are bringing children who are 'too old for story time' back to where they should be - to being kids.   Words can never express our gratitude or esteem we feel for you, Kerry. Thank you for every-thing you have given and continue to contribute to this project.

For Andy Kern, our engineer/producer extraordinaire! Your advice and suggestions for this venture are invaluable. Thank you for saying things like, "Let's record it again, Mrs. B. You just didn't sound like your usual perky self." You have corrected, admonished, encouraged, edified and consistently supported. Thank you for endless hours of work and your unfading commitment to this continuing endeavor.

In loving memory of Jan Marston
(She would be so proud of you, Kerry.)

Billy Bully Bug lived out on the farm.
He bullied in the day and the night.
He was the biggest bug on the farm
and gave all the other bugs a fright.

He hid in the bushes & jumped with surprise.
He frightened every bug to death.
He teased them and greased them
and egged them on and knocked
them really hard on their heads.

Billy Bully Bug was a mean ol' cuss.
Billy Bully Bug was a bum.
Billy Bully Bug scared all the little bugs
because he was a bigger bug.

Billy Bully Bug didn't waste any time.
He caused such panic and harm.
Enjoying his reputation as the meanest bad bug on the farm.

Billy Bully Bug would head off to school
beating up bugs on the way.
Taking their lunch money one by one,
he'd scare them all 'til they paid.

He ruined their books and tore their clothes,
knocked out some of their teeth.
He was the biggest bad ol' bug
any bug on the farm would ever meet.

Billy Bully Bug was
a mean ol' cuss.
Billy Bully Bug was a bum.
Billy Bully Bug scared all the little bugs
because he was a bigger bug.
Billy Bully Bug didn't waste any time.
He caused such a panic and harm.

Enjoying his reputation as the meanest bad bug on the farm.

8

Well, Billy Bully Bug
flew over the sea.
Let me be more specific.
He settled on an island in
the blue blue water in the
middle of the Pacific.
He landed on the pool on
the 7th floor at the
posh Honu LuLu Club.
He puffed up his chest,
stuck out his wings,
but he couldn't find
a single, little bug.

9

He flew into the weight room
and took a look around.
Before Billy knew what had happened to him,
he was flat face down on the ground.

He opened his eyes and
couldn't believe
towering way over him,
Rocky Rowdy Roach was
staring down at Billy and
Rocky Roach ruled the gym.

Billy Bully Bug was a mean ol' cuss.
Billy Bully Bug was a bum.
Billy Bully Bug scared all the little bugs.
He thought he was a bigger bug.
Billy Bully Bug didn't waste any time.
He had some lessons to learn.

13

To change his reputation as the meanest bad bug on the farm.

What Billy didn't know
was an issue of fact, a
necessary topic at hand.
Somewhere out there are
bugs bigger than you,
bugs born in the
tropical
lands.

Billy always thought that he was so bad,
then he took a better look all around.
He knew he'd better change the way that he was
or he'd spend a lot of time on the ground.

Yes, Billy Bully Bug was bigger than some.
Many bugs were two times his size.
Being a bully never ever even pays.
It took a bump on his
head to realize.
It took a bump on his
head to realize.

Billy Bug wasn't a mean ol' cuss.
He wasn't ever even a bum.
He didn't want to scare
all the little bugs.
He learned being scared
was no fun.

Billy Bug did not waste any time.
He never caused panic and harm.
He moved back to Minnesota with a
new attitude to be the nicest bug
on the farm.

WELCOME
TO
Minnesota

He moved back to Minnesota
with a new attitude to be the
nicest bug on the farm.

Coming Soon......

Juanita Maria Sophia Bug Diva©

Critters on the Farm©

My Sister and Me©

Lucia's Colorful World©

Katie Bug on the Farm©

The Nose Upon Your Face©

Holiday Land Lullaby©

(Listen to previews of these storybook songs
on our website.)

****

Other books currently in print.......

Bugs on the Farm©
Panuk, Princess and Prince (3-P's Piroshski Pit)©

(Order books online at www.mrsbstorytime.com or ask for them
at your local book store.)